For Jonathan and his big sister, Ellie, with love —S.L.-J.

For Sally Lloyd-Jones. —S.H.

All rights reserved. Published in the United States by Dragonfly Books, an imprint of Random House Children's Books, a division of Random House, Inc., New York. Originally published in hardcover in the United States by Schwartz & Wade Books, an imprint of Random House Children's Books, in 2007.

Dragonfly Books with the colophon is a registered trademark of Random House, Inc.

Visit us on the Web! www.randomhouse.com/kids

Educators and librarians, for a variety of teaching tools, visit us at www.randomhouse.com/teachers

The Library of Congress has cataloged the hardcover edition of this work as follows:
Lloyd-Jones, Sally.
How to be a baby—by me, the big sister / Sally Lloyd-Jones ; illustrated by Sue Heap.
p. cm.
Summary: An all-knowing big sister gives her baby sibling lessons in being a baby.
ISBN 978-0-375-83843-9 (trade) — ISBN 978-0-375-93843-6 (lib. bdg.)
[1. Babies—Fiction. 2. Sisters—Fiction.] I. Heap, Sue, ill. II. Title.
PZ7.J258Ho 2006
[E]—dc22
2006002469

ISBN 978-0-375-87388-1 (pbk.)

MANUFACTURED IN CHINA

10 9 8
First Dragonfly Books Edition

How to Be a BABY
by Me, The big sister
(and Sally Lloyd-Jones and Sue Heap)

Dragonfly Books ------- New York

When you're a baby,
you are in a crib and not
in school.

When you're a baby,
you just wear your pajamas ALL THE TIME
and not real clothes.

Your mommy and daddy
have to dress you,
because you don't know how.
(But I do.)

When you're a baby,
it's not good because
you don't have any hair.
(I have long hair like a princess.)

When you're a baby,
you don't read books.
You eat them.

You don't understand TV.

People talk to you,
but you don't know what it means.

You talk, but no one knows what you're saying,
because you just make it all up.

You sing songs,
but you don't know the words.
Or the tune.

(I know the words and the tune AND THE DANCE.)

When you're a baby,
you don't carry a backpack.
You go in one.

And you can only sit.
You can't stand,
or walk,
or go
ANYWHERE.

People have to carry you
EVERYWHERE.

(This is you being carried
EVERYWHERE.)

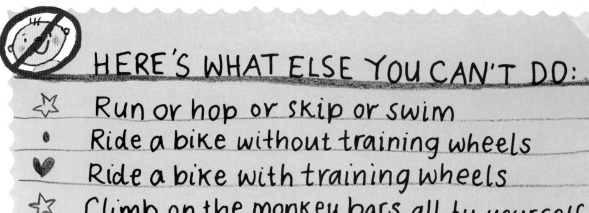

HERE'S WHAT ELSE YOU CAN'T DO:

- ☆ Run or hop or skip or swim
- • Ride a bike without training wheels
- ♥ Ride a bike with training wheels
- ☆ Climb on the monkey bars all by yourself
- • Bounce on the trampoline (it's SO EASY)
- ☆ Use scissors
- ♥ Be a princess or a fairy or a mermaid
- ! Actually anything really fun

When you're a baby,
your mommy and daddy have to feed you,
because you don't know how.

You don't have any teeth AT ALL.

You can't eat normal food.
You can only eat yucky baby food.

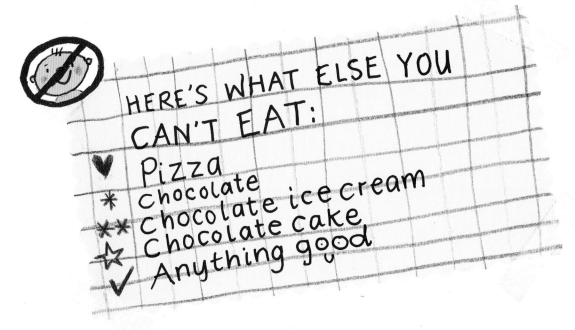

HERE'S WHAT ELSE YOU CAN'T EAT:

♥ Pizza
✳ chocolate
✳✳ Chocolate ice cream
☆ Chocolate cake
✓ Anything good

When you're a baby, you are scared of your potty.

HERE'S WHAT
ELSE YOU ARE
SCARED OF:

* The Ocean
! Grandma's Shiny
  Black Shoes
* The Easter Bunny
* Big Ted
* Actually lots of
  not-scary things
  at all

When you're a baby,
you're called Muffin or Pumpkin or Peanut or Dumpling,
and people say,

I could EAT you ALL UP !

But your real name is _____ .

(If you could write—which you can't—
you would put your name in that space.)

very small

When you're a baby,
you are very small.
People can hold you
in their hand, even.
Like a frog.

(This is you in someone's hand.)

Teeny weeny
eensy weensy
teeny tiny
baby!

When you're a baby,
you are a different shape.

You are round.

But then you get bigger
and your legs stretch out
and your tummy gets long
so you don't look so fat
like a big balloon
with a weird belly button
sticking out.

When you're a baby,
you don't know how old you are
or where you live
or even if you're a boy or a girl.

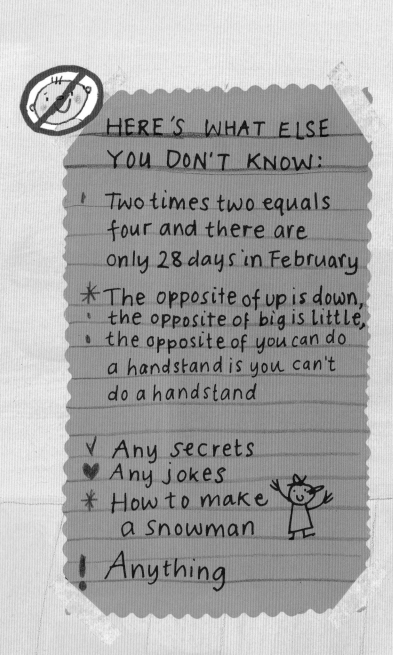

HERE'S WHAT ELSE
YOU DON'T KNOW:

- Two times two equals
  four and there are
  only 28 days in February

* The opposite of up is down,
  the opposite of big is little,
  the opposite of you can do
  a handstand is you can't
  do a handstand

✓ Any secrets
♥ Any jokes
* How to make
  a snowman

! Anything

I am a girl

MY BOOK of Anything

MY JOKES by me

I am 6

I live at this HOUSE

BIG elephant

UP

down

. ← little insect

Top Secret! KEEP OUT!!

When you're a baby,
baths are not nice.
They are dangerous.
Because you are too slippery
so someone has to watch you ALL THE TIME.

(This is me staying in the bath as long as I want all by myself.)

When you're a baby, it's not good
because the wind can blow you over.
When you're a baby, people eat your ice cream for you,
because ice cream isn't appropriate for babies.

And you're not allowed to TOUCH ANYTHING.

And a special plug goes in your mouth.
It's called a pacifier and it's to stop your scream coming out.

When you're a baby,
you don't sit on a chair.
You are tied to it.

Or you fall off and bang your head
and scream and have to go to bed.

And when you go in the car, you have to sit in a
baby-holder with a handle on it.
You don't even face the right way.

Facing
THE WRONG WAY

me
facing the right way

(I prefer to sit in a seat like a normal person.)

When you're a baby,
you have boring toys
like rattles and blocks.

HERE'S WHAT TOYS YOU DON'T HAVE
AND YOU'RE NOT ALLOWED TO PLAY WITH:

- ♥ My Bike
- ★ My Rollerblades
- ✳ My Game Boy
- ✓ My Playmobils because you might eat them
- ♥♥ My Ballerina Music Box
- ♥ All of my Barbies

When you're a baby,
you don't have good manners AT ALL.

You pull other people's glasses off,
and grab their noses,
and spit your food on them.

HERE'S WHAT ELSE
YOU DO THAT'S ILLEGAL:

★ Open other people's presents

! Knock other people's castles over

! Tear pages out of other people's favorite books

!! And scribble in them

X Draw on walls

!!! Poop on the carpet

X Other naughty things like that

Cats don't like you,
because you pull their tail,
and you pet their fur the wrong way.

Sometimes,
if you're VERY naughty,
you are put in prison.

(This is you IN PRISON.)

When you're a baby,
you don't have any real friends.
(I have lots.)

When you're a baby,
you have to have the light on ALL NIGHT
or you get scared.

And you're not allowed to have ANY pillows on your bed.

In the middle of the night,
you wake everyone up,
because you cry REALLY LOUD
and give me a headache.

And that's when I come in and
whisper to you and kiss you
and tell you, "Don't worry, Baby Dumpling,
it's just a scary dream," and then you feel better.

When you're a baby,
people hug you and kiss you
ALL THE TIME!

(Babies are good at hugging, but they can't kiss because
they don't know how their mouths work yet.)

HERE'S WHAT ELSE
BABIES ARE GOOD
AT:
★ Burping
! Peeing
!! Pooping
ᐯ Crying and screaming
zzz Sleeping
★ Making a mess

It's SOMETIMES nice being a baby
because people don't say,
"Stop being a BABY!"
Because you ARE a baby,
and you can't help it,
so it's not your fault.

And people smile at you because you're so small.

And sometimes you are funny
and you make me laugh.

When you get big,
you won't be a baby anymore.

But your mommy will still carry you if you're tired.
And your daddy will still sing songs
to you if you can't sleep.

And I will still let you hold my hand when you're afraid.
(Because you will still be a little bit little.)

HERE'S WHAT ELSE I'LL LET YOU DO:

* Follow me ✓
* Copy me ✓
* Play with my friends (sometimes) ✓
* Sit in my fort and have secrets together ✓
* Learn everything from me so you can be as smart and good at everything as me (almost) ✓

And ONE DAY
you'll be as tall as me!

And then I'll say,
"Remember when you were little? Remember?
How you used to never be able to do ANYTHING,
remember?"

And we'll laugh
and point at pictures of you in the olden days
when you were a baby.

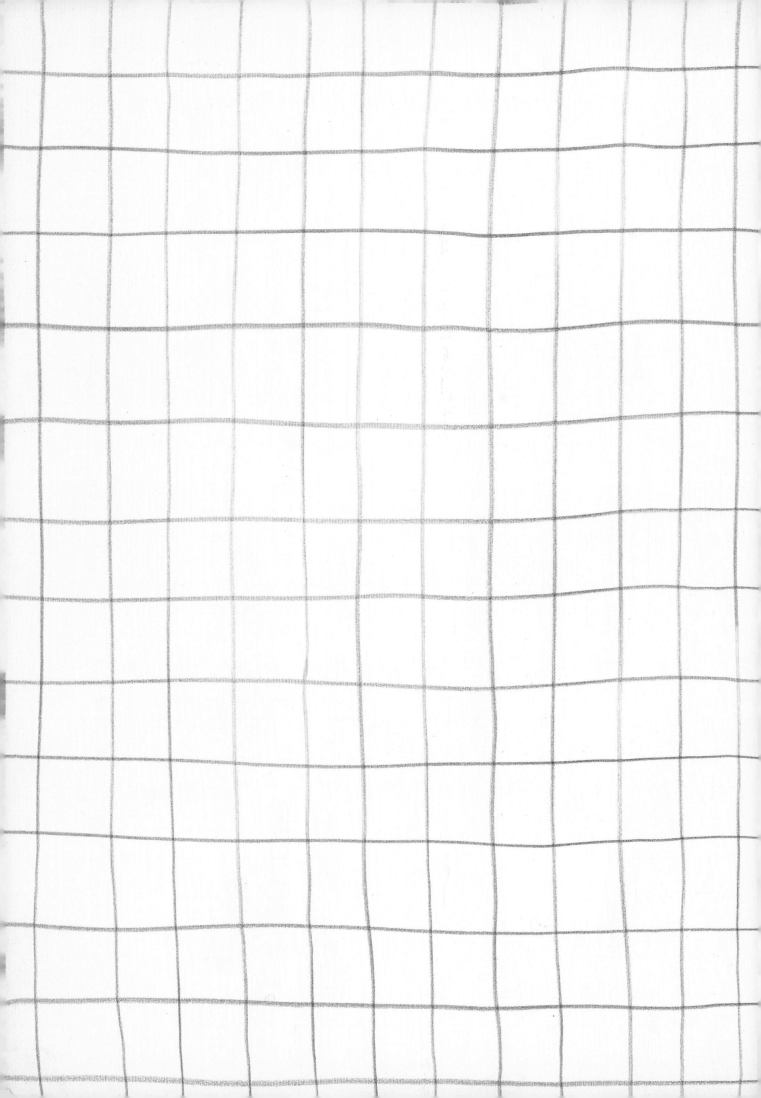